Smithsonian

LITTLE EXPLORER

DEINONYCHUS

by Joe Levit

CAPSTONE PRESS
a capstone imprint

Little Explorer is published by Capstone Press,
1710 Roe Crest Drive, North Mankato, Minnesota 56003
www.mycapstone.com

Library of Congress Cataloging-in-Publication Data

Names: Levit, Joseph, author.
Title: Deinonychus / by Joe Levit.
Description: North Mankato, Minnesota : Capstone Press, [2019]
| Series: Smithsonian little explorer. Little paleontologist |
Audience: Ages 6–7. | Audience: K to grade 3. | Includes
bibliographical references and index.
Identifiers: LCCN 2018043397| ISBN 9781543557480 (hardcover) |
ISBN 9781543560121 (pbk.) | ISBN 9781543557558 (ebook pdf)
Subjects: LCSH: Deinonychus—Juvenile literature. | Dinosaurs—
Juvenile literature.
Classification: LCC QE862.S3 L4845 2019 | DDC 567.912—dc23
LC record available at https://lccn.loc.gov/2018043397

Editorial Credits

Michelle Parkin, editor; Lori Bye, designer;
Kelly Garvin, media researcher,
Kathy McColley, production specialist

Our very special thanks to Matthew T. Miller, Museum Technician
(Collections Volunteer Manager), Department of Paleobiology at the
National Museum of Natural History, Smithsonian Institution, for his
review. Capstone would also like to thank Kealy Gordon, Product
Development Manager, and the following at Smithsonian Enterprises:
Ellen Nanney, Licensing Manager; Brigid Ferraro, Vice President,
Education and Consumer Products; and Carol LeBlanc, Senior Vice
President, Education and Consumer Products.

Image Credits

Alamy: Harold Smith, 20, Zuma Press Inc, 22; Jon Hughes, 1, 2, 5, 8-9,
10-11, 11 (bottom), 12-13, 14, 16-17, 19, 23, 24-25, 26, 30-31; Science
Source: De Agostini Picture Library, 18 (b), Nobumichi Tamura/
Stocktrek Images, 29 (top); Shutterstock: Anna Kucherova, 27,
Catmando, 16, die Fotosynthese, 18 (t), Herschel Hoffmeyer, 4 (b),
6-7, 16, 28, Michael Rosskothen, cover, Svetlana Eltsova, 9, tbob, 9,
Valentyna Chukhlyebova, 29 (b), Viktorya170377, 9, Zack Frank, 5 (b)

Printed and bound in the USA.
PA48

TABLE OF CONTENTS

name: Deinonychus

how to say it: die-no-NI-cuss

when it lived: early Cretaceous Period, Mesozoic Era

what it ate: meat

size: up to 11 feet (3.3 meters) long

3 feet (1 m) tall

weighed up to 220 pounds (99.7 kilograms)

Deinonychus belonged to a group of dinosaurs called theropods. Tyrannosaurus rex and Allosaurus were also members of this group.

Thanks to
FOSSILS

A fossil is evidence of life from the past. Fossil bones, teeth, and tracks found in the earth have taught us everything we know about dinosaurs.

Deinonychus skull

DEADLY DEINONYCHUS

triangle-shaped head

big eyes

large, grasping hands

three fingers on each hand

CHOMPING DOWN

Deinonychus had a wide head that was shaped like a triangle. There were 70 blade-like teeth inside its jaws.

Deinonychus had a strong bite for its size. It could rip flesh from bone.

One Big Bite

The force of an animal's bite is measured in newtons. Compare Deinonychus's bite to the bites of several modern animals.

spotted hyena:
566 newtons

American
black bear:
744 newtons

polar bear:
1,647 newtons

hippopotamus:
8,100 newtons

Deinonychus:
8,200 newtons

saltwater crocodile:
16,460 newtons

CLUTCHING CLAWS

Deinonychus had three clawed fingers on each hand. The dinosaur used its claws to grab prey.

Each foot had four toes. Deinonychus had a large sickle claw on the second toe of each foot. This claw was up to 5 inches (13 centimeters) long. It could be used to slash at other dinosaurs or cling to the backs of prey.

Deinonychus means "terrible claw."

PREHISTORIC BIRD OF PREY

Some scientists believe
Deinonychus used its
sickle claw to hold down
wiggly dinosaurs.

Modern birds of prey hunt this way. Hawks and eagles use their sharp talons to grab an animal. Then they stand on top of the prey. They dig their talons in deep. This keeps the animal from escaping.

FAST HUNTER

Scientists studied Deinonychus's tracks to learn how it moved. The dinosaur walked or ran on two legs. Deinonychus kept its sickle claw off the ground when it walked. This kept the large claw from catching on rocks and roots on the ground.

Deinonychus could walk about 6 miles (9.7 kilometers) per hour. It could run even faster. Deinonychus used its stiff tail for balance as it moved. The dinosaur could change directions quickly while chasing prey.

EARLY CRETACEOUS HOME

Deinonychus lived during the early
Cretaceous Period. It roamed through
what is now Montana, Wyoming,
Utah, and Oklahoma.

Deinonychus lived in warm forests.
It hunted along floodplains. The
dinosaur's swamplike habitat was
full of lagoons and tropical plants.

SAUROPELTA

TENONTOSAURUS

SAUROPOSEIDON

The Cretaceous Period lasted from 145 million to 66 million years ago.

DINOSAUR ERA

TRIASSIC	JURASSIC	CRETACEOUS

252   200   145   66   present

millions of
years ago

POSSIBLE PACK ANIMALS

Deinonychus was a carnivore. This means it ate meat. Scientists believe Deinonychus could have hunted in packs. This made it easier to take down large prey.

Deinonychus hunted giant dinosaurs such as Tenontosaurus. Scientists know this because Deinonychus teeth have been discovered near Tenontosaurus fossils. Scientists think a few Deinonychus would have been needed to attack the 4-ton dinosaur.

Some modern animals hunt in packs. Wolves form packs and attack larger animals such as moose and elk.

Zephyrosaurus

Deinonychus also hunted smaller dinosaurs such as Zephyrosaurus.

A Deinonychus skeleton is at the
American Museum of Natural
History in New York City.

DIGGING UP DEINONYCHUS

In 1931 paleontologist Barnum Brown discovered the first Deinonychus fossils in Montana.

More than 30 years later, paleontologists John Ostrom and Grant Meyer made an amazing discovery. While digging in Montana, they uncovered at least three complete Deinonychus skeletons.

Ostrom studied the bones as well as the fossils Brown had found years earlier. They were from the same type of dinosaur. Ostrom named Deinonychus in 1969.

BIRDS OF A FEATHER

While studying Deinonychus's bones, Ostrom noticed something unique. The dinosaur's hands and wrists could move sideways. Today's birds make this same motion to fly. This is one reason why scientists believe that modern birds are related to theropods such as Deinonychus.

A model of Deinonychus is at the San Diego Natural History Museum in California.

Like most theropods, Deinonychus probably had feathers. However, no real proof has been found to prove this.

NEST AND EGGS

In 2000 scientists found the first pieces of a Deinonychus egg. They were near the rib bones of an adult Deinonychus.

Scientists believe that Deinonychus could have sat on its eggs, as birds do today. Its body heat may have helped the dinosaurs inside the eggs grow.

Deinonychus eggs were 2.7 inches (7 cm) wide.

GROWING UP

Young Deinonychus didn't look like the adult dinosaur. They had longer arms and were probably covered in downy feathers.

Young Deinonychus may have eaten smaller prey such as lizards and insects. This is similar to reptiles today. Young Komodo dragons eat smaller prey such as snakes, birds, and insects. Adult Komodo dragons hunt large animals such as wild boars and deer.

Komodo dragon

THE RELATIVES

Several dinosaurs are related to Deinonychus. Some were small and others were very large.

Velociraptor was a small, feathered dinosaur. It was about 6.6 feet (2 m) long. It weighed about 33 pounds (15 kg). Velociraptor had a long skull and turned-up snout.

Deinonychus was used as the model for the Velociraptors featured in the *Jurassic Park* movies. Velociraptors were much smaller.

Dromaeosaurus was about the same size as Velociraptor. But it had a shorter and stronger jaw. It could run as fast as today's coyotes.

Utahraptor was much larger than Deinonychus. It was 19 feet (5.7 m) long. It weighed 1,100 pounds (500 kg). The dinosaur was about the size of a modern polar bear.

GLOSSARY

carnivore (KAHR-nuh-vohr)—an animal that eats only meat

floodplain (FLUHD-plane)—an area of low land near a stream or river that may flood

fossil (FAH-suhl)—evidence of life from the geologic past

habitat (HAB-uh-tat)—the natural place and conditions in which a plant or animal lives

Komodo dragon (KAH-moh-doh DRAG-uhn)—an Indonesian monitor lizard; Komodo dragons are the largest-known lizards in the world

lagoon (luh-GOON)—a body of water between the shore and a reef

Mesozoic Era (mehz-uh-ZOH-ik IHR-uh)—the age of dinosaurs that includes the Triassic, Jurassic, and Cretaceous periods, when the first birds, mammals, and flowers appeared

newton (NOOT-uhn)—a unit used to measure force

paleontologist (pale-ee-uhn-TOL-uh-jist)—a scientist who studies fossils

predator (PRED-uh-tur)—an animal that hunts other animals for food

prey (PRAY)—an animal that is hunted by another animal for food

serrated (SER-ay-tid)—saw toothed

sickle (SIK-uhl)—a sharp, curved edge that is shaped like the letter C

snout (SNOUT)—the long front part of an animal's head; the snout includes the nose, mouth, and jaws

talon (TAL-uhn)—a long, sharp claw

theropod (THAIR-oh-pod)—a member of a group of dinosaurs that walked or ran on two legs; most theropods ate meat

CRITICAL THINKING QUESTIONS

1. Deinonychus was a theropod. T. rex and Allosaurus were also theropods. Name two other dinosaurs that belonged to this group.

2. Deinonychus was used as the model for Velociraptor in the *Jurassic Park* movies. How are Deinonychus and Velociraptor similar? How are they different?

3. A relative of Deinonychus, Dromaeosaurus, could run as fast as a modern coyote. Go online and find out how fast a coyote can run.

READ MORE

Carr, Aaron. *Deinonychus.* Dinosaurs. New York: Smartbook Media, Inc., 2018.

Raymond, Jayne. *Meet Deinonychus.* The Age of Dinosaurs. New York: Cavendish Square Publishing, 2015.

Riehecky, Janet. *Velociraptor.* Little Paleontologist. North Mankato, MN: Capstone Press, 2015.

INTERNET SITES

Use FactHound to find Internet sites related to this book.

Visit *www.facthound.com*

Just type in 9781543557480 and go.

Super-cool stuff! Check out projects, games and lots more at **www.capstonekids.com**

INDEX